City
FOX

City FOX

by *Donna Bergman*

illustrated by *Peter E. Hanson*

Atheneum 1992 New York

Maxwell Macmillan International
New York · Oxford · Singapore · Sydney

Library of Congress Cataloging-in-Publication Data
Bergman, Donna.
    City Fox / by Donna Bergman; illustrated by Peter E. Hanson. —
1st ed.
        p.   cm.
    Summary: Ellie and Mrs. Kindley camp out one night to observe the
feeding habits of a fox.
    ISBN 0-689-31687-9
    [1. Foxes—Fiction.]   I. Hanson, Peter E., ill.   II. Title.
PZ7.B45222Ci   1992
[E]—dc20   90-27019

For my husband, Doug, who listens,
and for Jean Bryant, who inspires

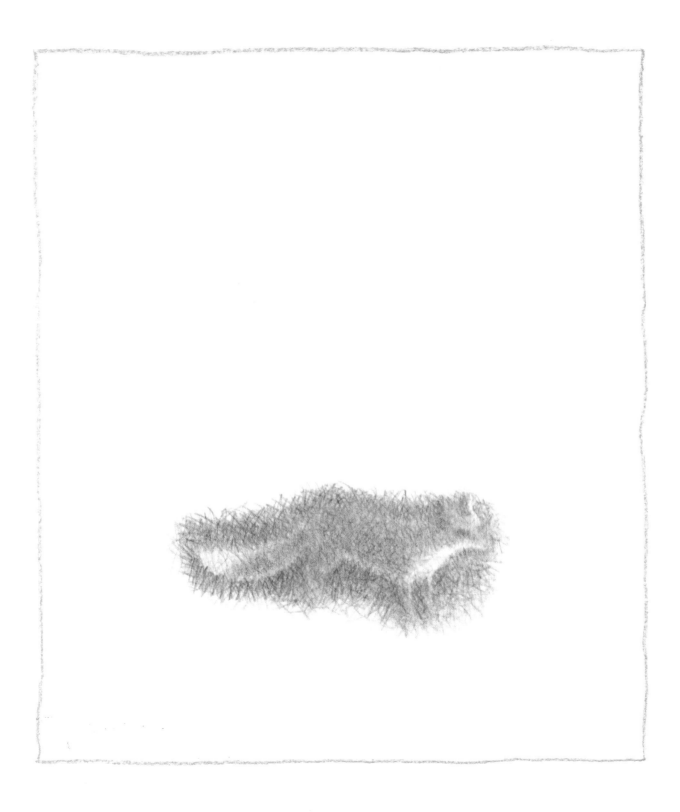

Most people think foxes live in the country, but sometimes foxes live in the city. Mrs. Kindley, my neighbor, had seen one. Lots of times. Late at night. I wanted to see him too.

Mrs. Kindley said City Fox—that's the name she called him—scooped out his den in the tangle of tree roots at the bottom of the hill behind our houses. Down where the soil is soft and sandy. Way beyond the apple tree and the pear tree and the plum tree. Down at the edge of the woods, where everything is quiet. Where I'm not allowed to play.

Every afternoon Mrs. Kindley walked down to the plum tree in her back garden and put food out for City Fox. He had a water bowl and a silver-colored pie plate that sat on a little platform under the tree.

Sometimes Mrs. Kindley let me go along and help feed City Fox. The first time, I remember, I had started to pour out dog food, when a plum fell down from the tree and landed in the pie plate with a loud *crash bang!* The noise scared me. I jumped straight up and yelled.

After that, I thought, Mrs. Kindley would never let me put out City Fox's food again. But she smiled at me and pointed to the plum. "City Fox likes fruit too," she said.

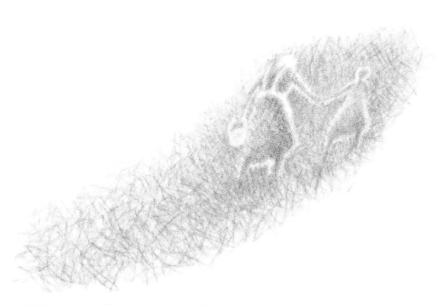

When the food was in the dish and the water in the bowl, we started up the hill. "What do foxes eat, besides dog food and plums?" I asked.

In between huffs and puffs, Mrs. Kindley said, "Foxes eat mice, if they can catch them. And insects. And chickens and eggs, if they're around. Why, they can even sniff out worms and then pull them from the ground all in one piece."

"Oh, ish," I said, but at the same time I wished I could see City Fox do that, so I asked, "Can I stay up some night and see City Fox?"

"Oh, Ellie," Mrs. Kindley said, "he comes long past your bedtime."

But my wish came true. One day Mrs. Kindley said to me, "Ellie, I'm getting too old to keep up this big house and yard by myself. I'm moving to an apartment."

I asked her if I could come visit. "Oh, yes!" she said with a smile, but then she looked grave and said, "It's not leaving this house that troubles me, it's leaving City Fox; he's come to depend on me. Who will take care of him when I'm gone?"

"I will," I told Mrs. Kindley, but she said, "You, Ellie? Oh, my goodness gracious. You're still too young."

All I could think about was City Fox and how sad Mrs. Kindley looked, so I drew pictures of City Fox. In one of the pictures I drew myself feeding him. I held the food right up close to City Fox's mouth.

Mother showed Mrs. Kindley my pictures. Mrs. Kindley looked at them a long time and then said, "Ellie, I think maybe you are old enough to feed City Fox, and you're old enough to stay up one night and see him!" I remember how excited I was.

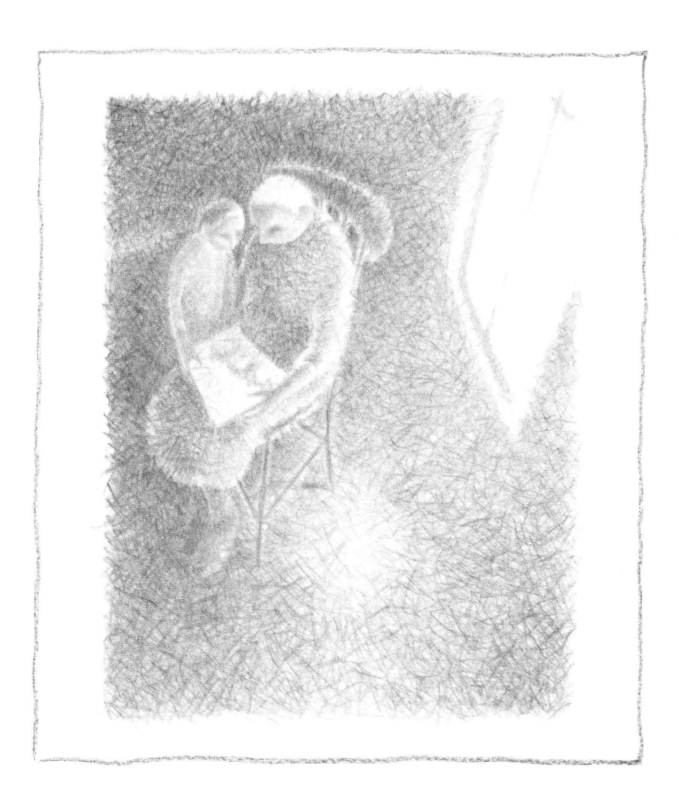

So one night near the end of summer, when everything was dry and crackly, Mrs. Kindley told me what I had to do. "It won't be easy, Ellie—you're still so young, and it's so late, but I know I can count on you."

Then she took my hand in hers and we went out into the darkness, where we huddled down together on the deck at the back of her house. I had to be very quiet. We were waiting for City Fox.

When we first settled down on the deck, Mrs. Kindley wrapped a quilt around us and we snuggled together. The quilt was warm, but still I shivered. I was thinking about City Fox.

I looked up at the night sky with the moon and all the stars and felt smaller than a speck of light from the farthest star. Mrs. Kindley put her arm around me and squeezed me. I stopped shivering.

Just then branches snapped in the garden below. Mrs. Kindley leaned forward and peered over the edge of the deck. I did too. It was dark out there, very, very dark.

City Fox was there; I knew he was. But I couldn't see him. And I couldn't ask Mrs. Kindley if she could see him, because I didn't want to scare him away. He hears much better than we do. And he's very shy. Mrs. Kindley told me that's why he eats at night.

Suddenly a spot of white shaped like a tiny flame appeared. It flickered back and forth. What was it? City Fox? The tip of his tail? That's what it was! It had to be. I was going to see City Fox!

But the white was sucked up by the darkness and everything grew quiet again. There was nothing more to see.

Why couldn't I have eyes like a fox? I wondered. Mrs. Kindley told me foxes have eyes like cats; they see really well in the dark.

Soon the moon, big and bright, climbed high in the sky. When it beamed down on the plum tree it made City Fox's pie plate gleam, like a second moon.

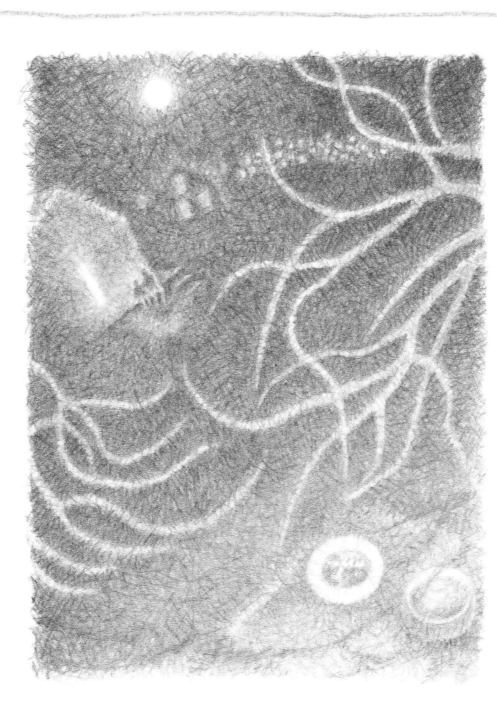

Would City Fox come back? I wondered. What was he doing? I tried to imagine what it would be like to hunt late at night for food. Did he search with fox friends or his fox family? Or was he all alone, like Mrs. Kindley?

All at once a little puff of wind set the wind chime at the end of Mrs. Kindley's deck to tinkling. Then from down below the deck I heard another sound, like when someone plops down on a pile of dry leaves. Sure it was City Fox, I listened for another sound. But there wasn't one.

Instead, it was very quiet. And the quilt was very warm. And my yawns felt as if they covered my face. I was afraid I'd fall asleep, but I had to stay awake.

So I twisted my head from side to side until, when I stopped, it felt like I was still doing it. I flung my head back and squinted at the moon. Then I pushed my chin against my chest and stared down at the pie plate.

I stopped wiggling, though, the minute Mrs. Kindley poked me. I thought she wanted me to sit still; instead, she wanted me to look where she was pointing.

City Fox!

He trotted along in a patch of moonlight. His reddish-colored coat gleamed as if from a thousand brushings. The sides of his nose and the tip of his tail gleamed white. I could barely breathe.

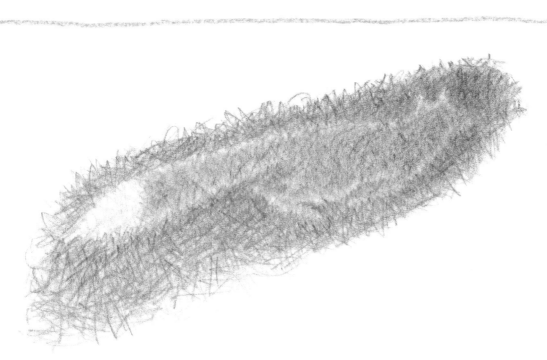

When he was close to the plum tree, he stopped and tilted his head. He seemed to be listening. Then he jumped onto the platform, where he gulped his food and drank his water. He licked his lips. A long time.

Before he jumped down, he looked up...right at me! His ears were pricked up; his eyes shone like little mirrors in the moonlight. I'm sure he was saying to me, "I know you're there." I smiled at him.

In an instant he turned and jumped back down. His long, bushy tail, almost as long as he was, sailed straight out behind him as he disappeared into the darkness.

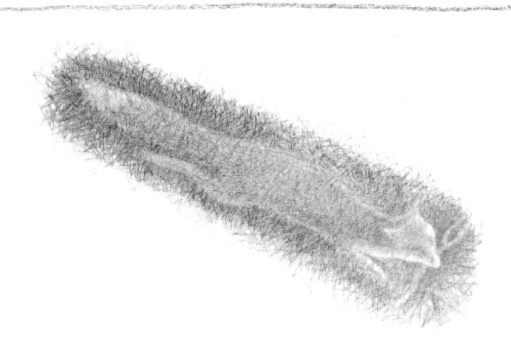

I stared at the spot where I last saw him; suddenly he came back. Running. He carried a stick in his mouth; he threw it into the air with a toss of his head. The stick flew way up. City Fox, like a dog chasing a Frisbee, dashed after the stick and grabbed it. He flung it up again. And again. Stopping and starting, going around in circles, even jumping straight up. He was being so silly I almost giggled.

The next time City Fox tossed his stick it fell into the shadows of the apple tree. He didn't go after it. Instead, he turned and trotted down the hill, toward the woods.

Mrs. Kindley and I waited. When he didn't come back, she said softly, "Do you think City Fox put on that show just for us, tonight, Ellie?"

"Oh yes!" I said, and sighed.

Later I thought about that special show every time I filled his dishes, and it made me smile.